For Milo
E.B.

For Helen Craig
D.P.

First published 1993 by Walker Books Ltd
87 Vauxhall Walk, London SE11 5HJ

Text © 1993 Eileen Browne
Illustrations © 1993 David Parkins

This book has been typeset in ITC Garamond.

Printed and bound in Hong Kong by
South China Printing Co. (1988) Ltd

British Library Cataloguing in Publication Data
A catalogue record for this book is available
from the British Library.

ISBN 0-7445-2205-6

No Problem

Written by
Eileen Browne

Illustrated by
David Parkins

CONSTRUCTION KIT

To Mouse,
Put together the things you see,
Then climb aboard and visit me!
Love from Rat

THIS WAY UP

WALKER BOOKS
LONDON

One morning, Mouse was woken up
by a heavy CLONK! outside her front door.
Whatever's that? Mouse thought. She
nipped out of bed, opened the door and
looked outside. In front of her was an
ENORMOUS parcel. It was wrapped in brown
paper and tied with string.

CONSTRUCTION KIT was stamped on the
front and a pink card hung from the side.
It read,

To Mouse,
Put together the things you see,
Then climb aboard and visit me!
Love from Rat.

"Oooooh!" squeaked Mouse.
She nibbled through the string,
peeled off the paper and
opened the parcel.

Inside was a mountain of bits and pieces –
just *waiting* to be put together.

Mouse sniffed them and snuffled them.
She poked them and prodded them.
"I can put these together," she said.
"NO problem."

To Mouse,
Put together the things you see,
Then climb aboard and visit me!
Love from Rat

CONSTRUCTION KIT
HOW TO PUT IT TOGETHER

She was in such a hurry to begin that she forgot to look for the instructions. She didn't see the sheet of paper which said,

CONSTRUCTION KIT.
HOW TO PUT IT TOGETHER!

Mouse set to work. She joined pipes here and fixed wheels there. She twisted and turned things. She fiddled and twiddled things. She bolted bolts and tightened nuts.

Then she stepped back to see what she'd made.

"Cor!" said Mouse. "What *can* it be?
It's a bit like a bike … but it isn't a bike.
I think I'll call it a Biker-Riker."
  She climbed on, started the engine and set off to see Rat.

The Biker-Riker was very jumpy and very wobbly.

It kept going on to one wheel and doing "wheelies" by mistake.

"Ooooh!" cried Mouse, hanging on tight. "Perhaps I haven't put it together quite right."

She was tottering along on one wheel, when she met Badger.

"Well, hello there, Mouse," growled Badger, peering over the top of her glasses. "What is that very peculiar *thing* you're riding?"

"It's a Biker-Riker," squeaked Mouse. "A construction kit. A present from Rat. I put it together, but it isn't quite right. It's very jumpy and very wobbly."

"Have you got the instructions?" asked Badger.

"No," said Mouse. "Can you help?"

Badger polished her glasses and blinked at the Biker-Riker. "Well now," she mumbled. "Let's see. Hmmmmmm."

Then she looked up and said, "I can fix this. NO problem."

Badger unscrewed the screws and unbolted the bolts. She shifted and shoved things. She changed and rearranged things. She reset the pipes and the wheels.

Then she stepped back to see what she'd made.

"Ahhh," said Badger. "What *can* it be? It's a bit like a car …
but it isn't a car. I think I'll call it a Jaloppy-Doppy."

"Come on," said Mouse. "Let's go to Rat's."

Mouse and Badger climbed in the Jaloppy-Doppy
and set off to see Rat.

The Jaloppy-Doppy was very bumpy and very rattly,

and not at all comfortable.

"Per-haps," said Badger, bouncing up and down, "I hav-en't put it to-ge-ther quite ri-ght."

They were juddering along a river bank, when they met Otter.

"Hey!" grinned Otter. "What the heck is that?"

"It's a Jaloppy-Doppy," snorted Badger. "A construction kit. Rat sent it to Mouse. I put it together, but it isn't quite right. It's very bumpy and very rattly."

"Got the instructions?" asked Otter.

"Sadly, no," said Badger. "Can you help?"

Otter dived into the Jaloppy-Doppy and rolled out again. She climbed up the front and slid down the back.

"I can fix this," said Otter. "NO problem."

She squeezed underneath and unbolted the bolts. She flipped bits and flopped bits. She switched bits and swapped bits. She moved all the wheels and she rebuilt the pipes.

Then she stepped back to see what she'd made.

"Wow!" barked Otter. "What *can* it be? It's a bit like a boat …
but it sure ain't a boat. I think I'll call it a Boater-Roater."

"Come on, then," said Mouse and Badger. "Let's go to Rat's."

Mouse, Badger and Otter pushed the Boater-Roater on to
the river. They jumped in and set off to see Rat.

The Boater-Roater kept rocking and rolling,

and letting in lots of water.

"*Geeeeee*," said Otter, swaying to and fro. "Perh*aaaaaa*ps I haven't put it tog*eeeeee*ther quite r*iiiii*ght."

They were sailing round a bend, when they met Shrew.

"Hi!" piped Shrew. "What's that?"

"It's a Boater-Roater," said Otter. "A construction kit. Rat sent it to Mouse. I put it together, but it ain't quite right. It keeps rocking and rolling."

"Have you got the instructions?" asked Shrew.

"No," said Otter. "Can you help?"

Shrew jumped into the Boater-Roater and scampered all over it. She peeped in corners, peered through pipes and peeked round poles. Then … she found something.

"YES!" said Shrew.
"I can fix this.
NO problem."

They pulled the Boater-Roater on to the river bank.

Shrew didn't

She *completely dismantled* the Boater-Roater.

And peeping down

"Pass me this!"
she ordered Mouse.

"Pass me that!"
she snapped at Badger.

"Give me those!"
she said to Otter.

switch bits,   or swap bits,   or flip bits,   or flop bits.

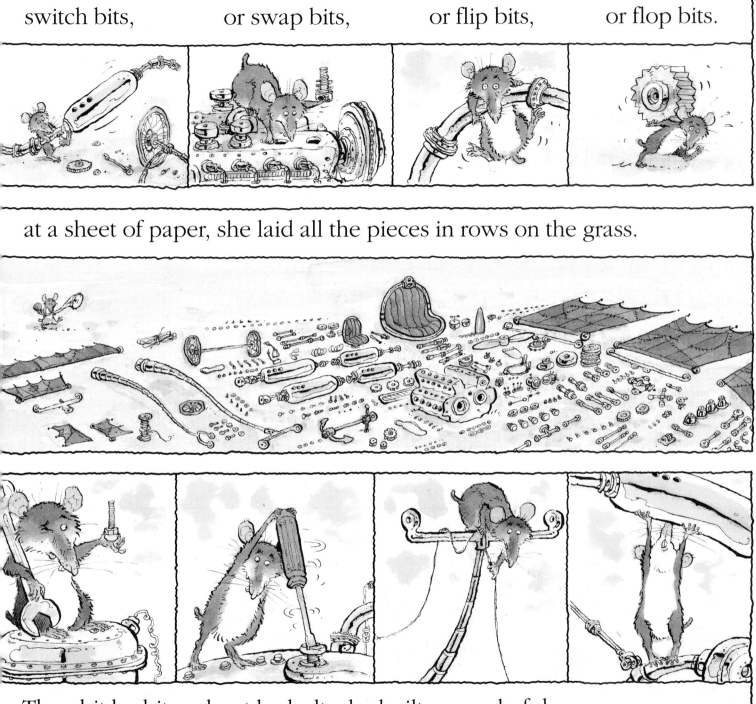

at a sheet of paper, she laid all the pieces in rows on the grass.

Then bit by bit and nut by bolt, she built a wonderful …

CONSTRUCTION KIT
(How to put it together)

AEROPLANE!

"How did you do it?" asked Mouse, Badger and Otter.

"Easy!" laughed Shrew. "I followed the instructions!" And she waved the sheet of paper that said,

CONSTRUCTION KIT.

HOW TO PUT IT TOGETHER!

"Well, I'll be blowed!" said the others. "Come on then, let's go to Rat's."

So Mouse, Badger, Otter and Shrew climbed into the aeroplane and set off to see Rat.

They raced across the grass and rose into the air.

"*Yoo-reeka!*" squeaked Mouse.

"*Yowler-rowler!*" growled Badger.

"*Bonanza!*" barked Otter.

"*Yazoo!*" piped Shrew.

The aeroplane didn't jump or wobble,
or bump or rattle, or rock or roll. It just flew
smoothly through the sky all the way to Rat's.

They landed the plane and climbed out.

"Look!" said Mouse. "There are balloons on Rat's door. She must be having a party."

The door swung open and out jumped Rat.

"HAPPY BIRTHDAY, MOUSE!" said Rat.

"Happy birthday," said Badger and Otter and Shrew. "Had you forgotten? It's your birthday! We're having a party."

"My birthday?" said Mouse. "Well I never!"

"I see you got the aeroplane," said Rat. "Did you have any trouble putting it together?"

Mouse winked at Badger. Otter winked at Shrew.
"Of course not," they said. "NO problem."